Undercover Explorer

Diana Herweck

Publishing Credits

Conni Medina, M.A.Ed., *Managing Editor*

Lee Aucoin, *Creative Director*

Diana Kenney, M.A.Ed., NBCT, *Senior Editor*

Christine Kinkopf, *Assistant Editor*

Hillary Dunlap, *Designer*

Rachelle Cracchiolo, M.S.Ed., *Publisher*

Image Credits: Cover, p. 1 Getty Images; p. 3 The Library of Congress [LC-D401-22452]; pp. 7–24 Bridgeman Art Library; all other images Shutterstock.

Teacher Created Materials

5301 Oceanus Drive
Huntington Beach, CA 92649-1030
http://www.tcmpub.com

ISBN 978-1-4807-4454-7

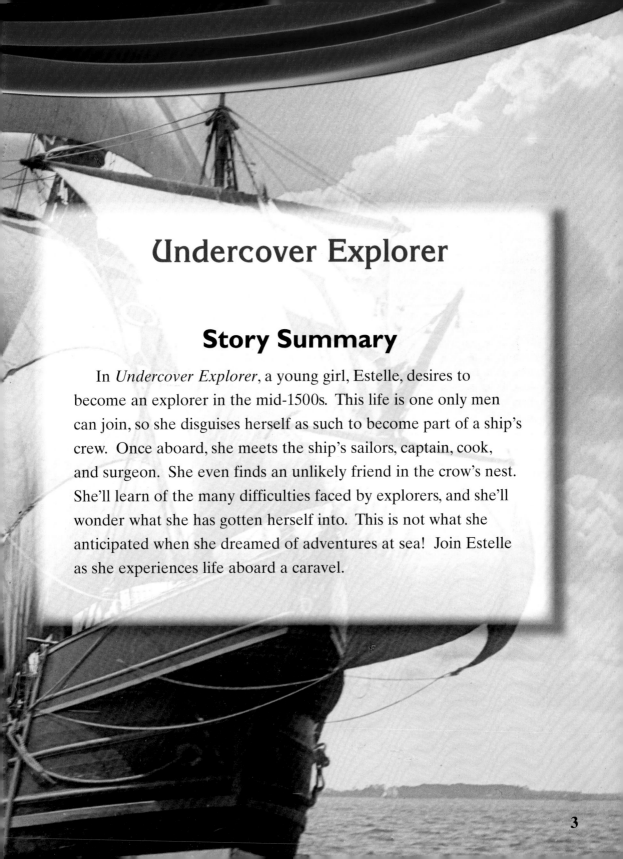

Undercover Explorer

Story Summary

In *Undercover Explorer*, a young girl, Estelle, desires to become an explorer in the mid-1500s. This life is one only men can join, so she disguises herself as such to become part of a ship's crew. Once aboard, she meets the ship's sailors, captain, cook, and surgeon. She even finds an unlikely friend in the crow's nest. She'll learn of the many difficulties faced by explorers, and she'll wonder what she has gotten herself into. This is not what she anticipated when she dreamed of adventures at sea! Join Estelle as she experiences life aboard a caravel.

Tips for Performing Reader's Theater

Adapted from Aaron Shepard

★ Don't let your script hide your face. If you can't see the audience, your script is too high.

★ Look up often when you speak. Don't just look at your script.

★ Talk slowly so the audience knows what you are saying.

★ Talk loudly so everyone can hear you.

★ Talk with feelings. If the character is sad, let your voice be sad. If the character is surprised, let your voice be surprised.

★ Stand up straight. Keep your hands and feet still.

Tips for Performing
Reader's Theater *(cont.)*

★ Remember that even when you are not talking, you are still your character.

★ If the audience laughs, wait for them to stop before you speak again.

★ If someone in the audience talks, don't pay attention.

★ If someone walks into the room, don't pay attention.

★ If you make a mistake, pretend it was right.

★ If you drop something, try to leave it where it is until the audience is looking somewhere else.

★ If a reader forgets to read his or her part, see if you can read the part instead, make something up, or just skip over it. Don't whisper to the reader!

Undercover Explorer

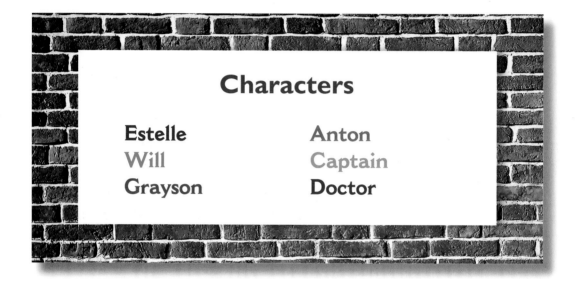

Characters

Estelle	Anton
Will	Captain
Grayson	Doctor

Setting

This story opens in the early 16th century, on a caravel heading to explore the New World. The caravel is small, but boasts a crow's nest, galley, head, and captain's quarters.

Act I

Will:	*(suspiciously)* Have you ever voyaged on a caravel before?
Estelle:	This is my first experience sailing on an expedition. Although, I have been on ships before . . . numerous times.
Will:	*(accusingly)* You look somewhat petite to be working on a caravel as a sailor.
Estelle:	I may appear petite, but I can manage. My family is filled with sailors. I want to learn everything I can before I am old enough to become an official sailor.
Will:	*(bragging)* I have been working on sailing boats since I was only 11. It's been a couple years now, and I will be made an official seaman when I'm 16. I have been on long expeditions before, but this journey is only supposed to take a couple months.
Anton:	Supper is ready, everybody! Time to get your grub!
Will:	Quick, let's hurry to the galley! Appetizing food will not be available very long with so many ravenous sailors on board. Plus, we do not usually have butter for our bread, but we will get some today.

❧❧

Anton:	Enjoy the dairy foods while you can because they will be rotten within a couple nights. Dairy doesn't last very long on this boat.

Estelle:	Are there any vegetables on this ship?
Anton:	No, vegetables also rot too quickly. It's much too damp to carry them aboard the ship. Any perishables that we carry must be eaten early during our journey; so, enjoy it all while it's available!
Will:	Since the fresh food disappears quickly, tell the newcomer what we will survive on during the latter months of our expedition.
Anton:	We normally eat biscuits, salted meat, oatmeal, and even dried peas when the fresh food is depleted. If anyone is lucky enough to catch fish, then we get to enjoy fresh seafood. Our goal is to consume at least one complete meal every day.
Estelle:	I hope someone catches fish today, seafood is my favorite!
Will:	We should return to the deck quickly. The captain is assigning watches to everybody, and we do not want to be absent to hear where we are needed.

Act 2

Grayson:	*(to himself)* Well, blow me over! There goes a very peculiar looking seafarer. I must remember to keep a steady eye on that tiny youngster.
Captain:	You're going to be separated into two watches on this expedition. You'll work four hours, and then receive four hours to rest and relax.

Will: *(whispering)* The sailors will get the best jobs, and we will get whatever assignments are remaining.

Captain: Each rotation will be assigned a cook, gunner, blacksmith, and carpenter.

Estelle: *(whispering)* What responsibilities does the blacksmith have on the ship?

Will: *(whispering)* He is the caretaker of the weapons. I imagine we have several cannons on this caravel. We always need to be prepared for pirates at sea or restless natives on land.

Estelle: *(loudly)* Goodness, I never thought about possible pirate attacks when I came aboard!

Captain: Youngsters, there are no private conversations while I'm giving orders. Now, with your undivided attention, I'll continue. We have only one barber, one astronomer, and one botanist aboard the vessel. They will rest when they are able and attend to their responsibilities when they are needed. The barber is also a trained surgeon. He will see to your medical needs. The astronomer will help with the ship's navigation, and the botanist will survey the plants we discover on our travels.

Estelle: *(whispering)* I hope the four-hour rest between watches will be sufficient.

Will: We should probably slumber anytime we get a chance; otherwise, we will not have enough energy, especially since it seems we won't be eating very much. Did your family not caution you about any of this?

Estelle: *(awkwardly)* I communicated my plans for this excursion with them.

Will: *(surprised)* You never considered the implications of this journey with them?

Captain: *(irritated)* There are two youngsters on each watch. You fellows will be responsible for swabbing the deck and cleaning the remainder of the caravel. You'll also be assisting other crewmen, when necessary. Perhaps some hard labor will remind you to show respect. We'll inform you when and where your assistance is needed, but you'll be expected to scour the deck, pump out seawater, and manage the sails. Your assistance to the surgeon, cook, and botanist will be indispensable. We'll also require your assistance in repairing the sails and lines, as well as taking watch in the crow's nest.

Will: Well, this is a predicament we have gotten ourselves into. Now that the captain is irritated with us, he will keep us extremely busy. Hopefully we can maintain good standing with the page and we will catch a break.

Estelle: *(sighing) Page*, another nautical word I do not understand; what exactly is a page?

Will: You do not know anything about sailing, do you? The page is the sailor who rotates the hourglass every half hour. Every time he does, the bell strikes. The eighth strike indicates the conclusion of a watch.

Song: Strike the Bell

Will: Sometimes the page rotates the hourglass earlier, though, granting people he favors with shorter watches.

Estelle: That hardly seems equitable to the other sailors who will get less rest. I better hurry to work now, but I would like to go up in the crow's nest to have a look first.

꿎꿎

Grayson: Come right up, newcomer. My name is Grayson. Just scramble on up that tall, swinging ladder and you'll behold the most spectacular and amazing panorama you've ever seen. Proceed cautiously, though, and watch your step.

Estelle: I have never ascended such a tall ladder before, and I am a little apprehensive about heights. Whoa! It is pretty shaky climbing up here.

Grayson: Yessiree, and if you misplace your footing, you'll be finding yourself descending all the way back to the deck. The wind will be blowing strongly when you get to the top, and you'll surely feel what the sails feel, so hang on tight.

Estelle: *(amazed)* I have finally reached the top! What a breathtaking horizon! There is ocean extending far into the distances. It appears as though I am sitting on top of the world.

Grayson: The view is definitely beautiful up here, but unfortunately there is no time for relaxing. The sailor in the crow's nest has an important task: he must watch for dangers at sea, including pirate ships and other hazards. Keep your eyes open, and if you see any danger or if you see land, alert the captain right away.

Estelle: *(distracted)* Is that singing coming from somewhere on the ship?

Grayson: The melody you're hearing is a sea shanty. The sailors are humming and singing ditties as they attend to their tasks. It helps them pass the time, and the rhythm of the songs help the crewmen synchronize their movements, so they get their work done quicker and more efficiently.

Estelle: *(nauseated)* I am beginning to feel queasy up here, Grayson.

Grayson: That's not uncommon. Many sailors get seasick in lofty elevations like the crow's nest. The movements of the ship are actually amplified at this higher altitude. After all, you're almost 100 feet up. Sometimes the captain assigns the crow's nest to a sailor as punishment, requiring the sailor to remain here watch after watch. Most sailors refuse to admit they feel sick, but you're different . . . *(suspiciously)* You don't seem like a typical sailor.

Estelle: *(quickly)* Thank you for the company, Grayson! It is imperative I return to the deck now. I have obligations down below.

Act 3

Anton:	Hurry, hurry! I need your assistance in the galley. We should already be preparing the next meal!
Estelle:	What are we preparing for supper tonight?
Anton:	We'll be preparing meat and hardtack biscuits. The meat has been salted and dried, so it's already well preserved and should last us throughout the lengthy expedition. When we exhaust our entire supply of meat, we still have suet. We use suet to make hardtack, which are biscuits made of flour, water, and salt. They might not taste very delicious, but they fill our stomachs and store well for the months we're sailing at sea.
Estelle:	Is there anything to drink tonight?
Anton:	We have nearly a gallon of grog for each sailor every day. Sometimes, we'll combine the grog with water to allow it to stretch further. Because the water and alcohol are mixed together, the water won't develop algae. Water usually doesn't last us very long on these voyages anyway. Enough talking now, I need you to scamper down below deck to gather some more biscuits for the sailors.

෨෧

Estelle: I am finally back! I apologize that it took so long; I had difficulty finding the specific items you requested. I located this flour and these biscuits, but they contain little bugs. These cannot possibly be the items you requested.

Anton: You're getting awfully picky there, youngster. Weevils and other insects burrow into our food supply, and there's nothing we can do to prevent it. *(laughing)* But don't worry, a little extra meat in your diet won't hurt you!

Estelle: Am I really expected to eat these vulgar bugs?

Doctor: *(joining the conversation)* If you're going to inhabit this caravel for several months, you certainly are. Measly insects aren't what you should be worried about, anyhow. There are countless other dangers aboard the ship.

Estelle: What other dangers exist aboard this ship?

Doctor: Deadly diseases from rats and vermin are a few. Not to mention scurvy and outside dangers like malicious pirates.

Estelle: *(abruptly)* The page's bell is finally striking, so my watch has concluded. I should probably attempt to slumber before my next shift. Can you direct me to our sleeping quarters?

Anton: You can sleep down below where the food and other provisions are stored. When it becomes warmer, the crew usually spreads out around the upper deck, but for now you must stay below. I'll see you when we prepare the next meal.

Grayson: *(to himself)* That newcomer has a weaker stomach than most on this vessel. I can't figure out what's different about him, but he's definitely unique. He doesn't seem prepared for what this expedition will bring. I wonder what he's doing here . . .

❧∾❧

Estelle: It is incredibly crowded in here, Will. All the hammocks are occupied, and there is no comfortable place for me to slumber.

Will: You should probably sit on the lines over there and attempt to sleep.

Estelle: I want to avoid positioning myself too closely to the flour bags in that corner, as the weevils in the flour are disgusting!

Will: Well, you have probably already noticed, but we share the area with a multitude of rats and other vermin. There simply is not enough space to be alone.

Estelle: I think this journey is a more strenuous adventure than I bargained for.

Will: *(mockingly)* Oh, you are a sailor who only considered the excitement of the journey without considering the difficulty of the work or the associated risks. Well, prepare yourself: there are a multitude of dangers! I thought you have experienced sailors in your family. If you had told them your intentions, they would have warned you.

Estelle: They would not have allowed me to join the expedition. They would have encouraged me to join the navy in several years, but I did not want to postpone my adventures any longer. *(changing the subject)* It is essential that I get some rest now.

Act 4

Doctor: It's practically time to initiate your next watch, and it's imperative that you youngsters provide assistance on deck. Did you get adequate rest?

Estelle: Not really. It was extremely stuffy below deck, and I am still quite nauseated from the ship's rolling motion.

Doctor: Your condition doesn't surprise me. Everybody sleeps better when the weather's friendlier and they can spread about on deck. The area below is stuffy and overcrowded with all of the food, supplies, and unwanted vermin, it's miserable down there.

Estelle: There is not exactly privacy down there either!

Doctor: No, privacy is not a top priority on a caravel. Another piece of advice: always be aware of the sails. Many times, onlookers must adjust position to allow for safe maneuvering of the sails. If you aren't paying attention, you may end up with a large, unsecured beam swinging over your head while you sleep.

Will: It would be terrible to have a massive wooden beam knock you senseless!

Estelle: How am I supposed to focus on my watches when I am always thinking about the sails?

Doctor: Sails are the least of your worries, anxious youngster. During my last expedition, nearly half the crew suffered from horrifying diseases. Like the captain said, I'm not only a barber, but also a surgeon. I treat bedridden sailors, attempting to alleviate their discomfort and cure their diseases. Unfortunately, some actually die. We don't want disease to spread; consequently, we must remove the bodies from the ship. So, we fasten the deceased bodies into sewn sacks and lower them into an oceanic grave.

Estelle: What causes the deadly diseases?

Doctor: It's difficult to say. I know what causes my constant discomfort though. As you have likely noticed, most of us only have one set of clothing. We wear those clothes every day and night. We also don't have many opportunities to wash our garments. The combination of soiled clothes and filthy bodies, especially when living in cramped quarters, results in many complications. Extreme itching and discomfort make other diseases that much more uncomfortable.

Estelle: What other diseases?

Doctor: Typhoid fever, for example.

Will: Maybe we should explain to him the many precautions we take to avoid these problems.

Doctor:	Well, we can't bathe or swim in the ocean water due to its cold and dangerous nature. However, we can fill buckets with water and splash ourselves while on board. Of course, the water is extraordinarily frigid, which results in fast baths and inadequate cleaning. When the weather is warmer, we launder the bedding and hammocks, as well as our clothing, and hang them to dry. This helps decrease infestations of problematic lice and bugs.
Will:	Tell him about the filthy vermin we observed down below.
Doctor:	It's really impossible to eradicate the vessel of all of them, especially with the food and provisions below. We do have a cat on board, though, and he does what he can to get the rats.
Will:	*(sighing)* I already hear the bell striking. We better hurry to our next watch; we have many responsibilities to attend to.
Estelle:	*(interjecting)* But before heading to work, I must find the lavatory.
Doctor:	The head is located at the bow, or front, of the caravel. Its forward location is our meager attempt to maintain a sanitary vessel. The ocean water splashes aboard and washes away the residual waste. It's not much of a solution, but the vulgar smell dissipates a little.

Act 5

Anton:	Ah, my two helpers have finally arrived to help me prepare our next meal. Some of the sailors caught fish, so we will prepare seafood this evening. We're going to prepare soup for tomorrow with the tablets the captain brought aboard.
Will:	What tablets? In my numerous years on caravels, I have never heard anything about tablets.
Anton:	I have been searching for ways to improve the health of our sailors while on the ship. We can't keep vegetables on board, so we're trying tablets made of dried vegetables. We hope that we will be able to prevent diseases, such as scurvy, by having better food options.
Estelle:	The doctor mentioned it before, but what exactly is scurvy?
Anton:	It's a vicious disease that will make you wish you'd stayed home. I've heard it makes you short of breath and your limbs are in constant aching agony. Your teeth start to rot and eventually fall out. It will even alter your hearing and vision. A gunshot sound is enough to kill a man dying of scurvy.
Will:	That sounds like an excruciating way to die.

Poem: The Sailor Boy

Captain: All hands on deck immediately! We've had enough toiling for the day. It's about time we enjoy some amusing entertainment!

Estelle: How exciting! What activities are there?

Captain: Many of the sailors like to participate in dice and card games, but several play musical instruments. Some of the sailors play tabors and pipes, while others play accordions and fiddles. There is an abundance of music aboard this vessel. Many crewmen enjoy drawing and carving, and others practice knotting and model making. One of the most popular games on the ship is Nine Men's Morris. We frequently find ourselves telling stories and reading, too.

Will: What about gambling? I have heard there is often an abundance of gambling on these expeditions.

Captain: Many sailors turn to gambling to occupy their time, but it is not permitted on my caravel. If you do so, you will find yourself facing a considerable amount of punishment. You must follow the policies on board or there will be consequences to pay.

Will: This newcomer already knows about the punishment in which sailors are assigned to the crow's nest. What are some other types of punishment?

Captain: Sailors who have committed offenses have been savagely hanged, swung overboard, and even dragged in the water under the ship. I'm positive you can imagine some don't survive such torture. Some sailors are beaten with a cat o' nine tails. Trouble is not tolerated on this ship, and punishment is severe.

Estelle: Rest assured, I am not planning on causing any trouble. I would, however, like to learn the game you mentioned, and I would love to peruse a novel, if I can locate one on the vessel. In the meantime, though, I think I will head up the crow's nest to visit Grayson.

❧

Grayson: Welcome back, youngster. I was convinced you wouldn't be visiting me again, since you were so nauseated earlier.

Estelle: This looks like a perfect location to enjoy some peace and quiet and contemplate my situation. I do not know what I was thinking when I came aboard.

Grayson: Confide in me regarding why you chose to join the expedition.

Estelle: I thought it sounded like an adventure. I thought it would be a couple months filled with excitement. Nobody ever told me about the difficult work and the many dangers, including death.

Grayson: Don't you have experienced sailors in your family?

Estelle: Honestly, nobody in my family has ever sailed. I never considered the endless amount of work there would be; instead, I was just expecting to see the world. I am actually only 12 years old and . . . I am a girl. I disguised myself as a boy so I could get on the ship, and my disguise was not even that believable. Please refrain from saying anything to the others, Grayson!

Grayson: Aha! I supposed there was something unusual about you. Mystery solved . . . *(winking),* but you needn't worry, your secret's safe with me!

The Sailor Boy

by Lord Alfred Tennyson

He rose at dawn and, fired with hope,
    Shot o'er the seething harbour-bar,
And reach'd the ship and caught the rope,
    And whistled to the morning star.

And while he whistled long and loud
    He heard a fierce mermaiden cry,
"O boy, tho' thou are young and proud,
    I see the place where thou wilt lie.

"The sands and yeasty surges mix
    In caves about the dreary bay,
And on thy ribs the limpet sticks,
    And in thy heart the scrawl shall play."

"Fool," he answer'd, "death is sure
    To those that stay and those that roam,
But I will nevermore endure
    To sit with empty hands at home.

"My mother clings about my neck,
    My sisters crying, 'Stay for shame;'
My father raves of death and wreck,
    They are all to blame, they are all to blame.

"God help me! save I take my part
    Of danger on the roaring sea,
A devil rises in my heart,
    Far worse than any death to me."

Strike the Bell

Traditional

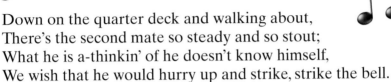

Down on the quarter deck and walking about,
There's the second mate so steady and so stout;
What he is a-thinkin' of he doesn't know himself,
We wish that he would hurry up and strike, strike the bell.

Strike the bell second mate, let us go below;
Look well to windward you can see it's going to blow;
Look at the glass, you can see that it is fell,
Oh we wish that you would hurry up and strike, strike the bell.

Down on the main deck and workin' on the pumps,
There is the starboard watch just longing for their bunks;
Look out to windward, and see a great swell,
And we wish that you would hurry up and strike, strike the bell.

Forward at the forecastle head and keepin' sharp lookout,
There is Johnny standin', a longin' for to shout,
"Lights are burnin' bright sir and everything is well."
We wish that you would hurry up and strike, strike the bell.

Aft at the wheel house, old Anderson stands,
Graspin' at the helm with his frostbitten hands,
Looking at the compass and the course is clear as well,
He's wishin' that the second mate would strike the bell.

Aft on the quarter deck our gallant captain stands,
Lookin' out to sea with a spyglass in his hand.
What he is a-thinkin' of we know very well.
He's thinking more of shortenin' sail than striking the bell.

This is an abridged version of the complete song.

Glossary

caravel—a small 15th and 16th century sailing ship

cat o' nine tails—a whip made of nine knotted cords fastened to a handle

crow's nest—a platform with short walls that is high on a ship's mast and from which you can see things that are far away

galley—a ship's kitchen

grog—an alcoholic drink

head—a ship's toilet

lines—long and thin ropes

Nine Men's Morris—an old board game, often played on ships

scurvy—a disease that is caused by not eating enough fruits and vegetables that contain vitamin C

shanty—a song that sailors sang in the past while they worked

suet—a type of hard fat that is found in cows and sheep

tabors—small drums used as musical instruments

Typhoid fever—a disease that is caused by a bacterium, is characterized by fever, diarrhea, weakness, headache, and an inflamed intestine, and is passed from one person to another through contaminated food or water

vermin—small insects and animals, such as fleas or mice, that are sometimes harmful to plants or other animals and that are difficult to get rid of

weevils—small insects that eat grains and seeds and that can ruin crops